Anxious Annie

Other Books by Leo Zarko

For Children:

Dorothea the Dog Rescuer
Rupert's Happy Home
My First Fish
Safety Squirrel
Farah Wants to Fly
Mory the Mouse
Sidney the Songbird
Wendy the Weed
Cozy & Zeno
Pauley's Piano
Arty the Artist
The Animals And The Mirror
The Visiting Cat

Poetry:

Something About Me
Just a Thought
From Me to You
Drifting
Searching

Anxious Annie

Written by Leo Zarko
Illustrated by Laura Reyes

Bringing Joy to Others is a Gift.

Give it Often!

God Bless

Anxious Annie's hair was the color of strawberries and her eyes were as green as the grass.

Annie was in grade school and often found herself anxious in class.

She had trouble sitting still in her chair and most of the time she would wiggle.

When the teacher called on her some of her classmates would stare at her and giggle.

"Why am I so anxious?" Annie would often ask her mother.

Her mother always replied the same, "You're a young child full of energy. So that makes you no different from any other."

Annie liked that answer as she skipped off to play.

But after hours of fun, she was still wound up at the end of the day.

The neighbors next door had a swimming pool and Annie was often their guest.

She wasn't the best swimmer, but she certainly tried her best.

The neighbors had a son, and together he and Annie would jump to see who could make the biggest wave.

His name was Cameron and he found Annie to be quite funny when she didn't behave.

Cameron helped Annie with her homework because he was smart like that.

Sometimes he would climb a tree to help bring down Annie's cat.

When the pair took bicycle rides Cameron rode slowly while Annie rode fast.

He was okay with her winning and didn't mind coming in last.

Cameron's parents would take him fishing and he liked it when Annie tagged along.

Everyone would sing out loud and they laughed when Annie got the words wrong.

If the fish weren't biting, Annie would dance and skip stones across the lake.

Cameron would ask her to stop and say, "You're scaring the fish, for goodness sake!"

Annie had a tooth ache one morning, but she was a bit too nervous to sit in the dentist's chair.

All she could think about was the sound of little drills and the smell of toothpaste in the air.

She told her mom she didn't want to go as she yelled and stomped her feet.

But her mother told her, "Honey, it's not going to hurt, plus when the dentist is done you'll get a sticker and a treat."

Riding the bus was another thing Annie didn't like to do.

She thought the kids were too loud and acted like wild monkeys at the zoo.

She was lucky because Cameron helped her each day on their ride to school.

He was right by her side, always calm and always cool.

Annie's mom liked to bake large cakes with lots of frosting on top.

While she baked she listened to music and watched Annie dance non-stop.

But at the end of the day, Annie's energy was always somewhat high.

So right before bedtime her mother taught her to relax by counting stars in the sky.

For the school play this year Annie felt brave and tried out for the lead role!

She liked acting because she could feel it deep down in her soul.

When try-outs arrived, Annie got anxious while standing on stage.

Somehow she had forgotten all the lines written on the page!

Lucky for her they told her she could come back the next day and try again.

But she was still shook up even after counting to ten.

Cameron told Annie not to throw a fit.

"When you try out tomorrow," he said, "you're going to be a big hit."

In front of Cameron, Annie didn't feel so shy and scared.

She was glad to have such a great friend who cared.

Cameron told her to remember how the stars made her feel at night.

He said, "That way when you read, you'll remember to feel alright."

When Annie woke the next morning she remembered what Cameron had said.

All day she stayed calm and counted the little stars in her head.

Annie did a great job reading, even better than expected!

She said her lines perfectly and this time wasn't rejected!

Getting off stage she smiled from ear to ear.

She was so thrilled knowing that she had conquered her fear.

The night of the play Cameron painted stars on a poster and sat in the front row.

Annie was fantastic and her parents gave her flowers after the show.

Cameron cheered, "You did it! You played your part perfectly until the end!"

Annie gave Cameron a huge hug and said, "I'm so grateful to have such a wonderful friend!"

The next day Annie thought to herself, *Why doesn't Cameron seem anxious or ever in a hurry?*

He rarely gets upset and he doesn't seem to worry.

Annie thought, *There must be a secret,* and of course she needed to know.

Cameron, sitting on the grass, replied, "I get anxious too, I just don't let it show."

"My grandpa didn't say much, so when he talked it was something he wanted me to know."

Cameron said his grandpa would say things like, "When the world gets going too fast, that's when you need to go slow."

He believed in his grandpa because he was brave and wise from living so many years.

He said his grandpa talked about pushing forward despite any fears.

"Like the night passes into the day, feelings are just feelings and they tend to go away."

Cameron remembered those words and he remembered them clear.

He felt fortunate to have such a great grandpa that helped him with his fear.

To celebrate the play, the kids went to the amusement park.

Cameron didn't want to admit it, but the rides seemed really scary in the dark.

"Come on, Cameron, I promise it'll be fun."

Cameron laughed because now it was his turn to be the anxious one.

Annie picked the biggest ride and asked Cameron to ride along.

She could see he was in need of a distraction, so she started singing him a song.

He immediately felt better and said, "We help each other out and that's a great thing."

That's when she smiled at her best friend and they both started to sing.

Made in the USA
Monee, IL
23 December 2020